Clifford THE BIG RED DOG®
THE BIG LEAF PILE

Adapted by Josephine Page
Illustrated by Jim Durk

Based on the Scholastic book series "Clifford The Big Red Dog" by Norman Bridwell

From the television script
"Leaf of Absence" by Scott Guy

SCHOLASTIC INC.
New York   Toronto   London   Auckland   Sydney   Mexico City
New Delhi   Hong Kong   Buenos Aires

ISBN 0-439-21357-6

It was a beautiful fall day
on Birdwell Island.
Cleo, Clifford, and T-Bone
were making leaf piles.

Cleo finished her pile

of leaves. They were red, yellow,

orange, gold, and brown.

She counted—

one, two, three—

and jumped in.

Clifford finished his pile

of leaves. They were red, yellow,

orange, gold, and brown.

He counted—

one, two, three—

and jumped in.

T-Bone's pile was not

finished yet. T-Bone's pile

had only brown leaves. Brown

leaves make a nice, loud sound.

"I need more leaves,"

T-Bone said.

"I will help," said Clifford.

"I will help, too," said Cleo.

And they did.

T-Bone's pile of
leaves was ready.
But T-Bone had to go home.
It was time for him
to go for a walk.

"I will watch your leaves,"
said Clifford. "They will
be safe with me. I promise."

"You are a good friend,"

said T-Bone.

And a happy T-Bone trotted off.

Clifford watched the pile

of leaves. He watched

and watched some more.

"This is a very nice leaf pile,"
he said. "I can't wait to hear
its loud sound."
"We could jump in carefully
so we don't mess it up," said Cleo.

"Yes, we could," said Clifford.

"Then let's jump," said Cleo.

The leaves flew.

A strong wind blew them

everywhere.

"Oh, no!" said Clifford.

Clifford and Cleo chased

T-Bone's leaves.

One leaf was

on a weather vane.

Another leaf was

under the mail truck.

Clifford and Cleo found a leaf

on a swing in the playground.

They found a leaf
on some french fries.

Clifford and Cleo found every
one of the missing leaves.

"This is a great leaf pile,"

said Clifford.

"I can't wait to hear

the noise it makes," said Cleo.

"We could jump in,"

Clifford said.

"But we won't,"

they said together.

T-Bone came back.

His pile looked even bigger
and better than before.

"Thank you for watching

my leaves," he said to Clifford.

"I want you to be the first

to jump in."

"We must tell you the truth.

We already jumped into your pile.

All your leaves flew away,"

Clifford said. "But Cleo and I got

them back. I'm sorry, T-Bone."

"I'm glad you told me the truth," said T-Bone. "I still want you to jump in first."

So Clifford jumped in

with a big *CRUNCH!*

Then Cleo and T-Bone jumped in.

CRUNCH! CRUNCH!

And the three friends enjoyed
the rest of the beautiful
fall day.

Do You Remember?

Circle the right answer.

1. The names of the characters in the story are...
   a. Clifford, Nero, and T-Bone.
   b. Clifford, Cleo, and T-Bone.
   c. Clifford, Nero, and T-Shirt.

2. T-Bone's leaves are...
   a. red, yellow, gold, and brown.
   b. all yellow.
   c. all brown.

Which happened first?
Which happened next?
Which happened last?
Write a 1, 2, or 3 in the space after each sentence.

T-Bone had to go home. _____

T-Bone made
a brown leaf pile. _____

Clifford and Cleo found a leaf
under a mail truck. _____

Answers:

Clifford THE BIG RED DOG®

THE DOG WHO CRIED "WOOF!"

Adapted by Bob Barkly

Illustrated by John Kurtz

**Based on the Scholastic book series
"Clifford The Big Red Dog"
by Norman Bridwell**

From the television script "The Dog Who Cried 'Woof'"
by Anne-Marie Perrotta and Tean Schultz

Cartwheel
·B·O·O·K·S·®

SCHOLASTIC INC.

New York   Toronto   London   Auckland   Sydney   Mexico City
New Delhi   Hong Kong   Buenos Aires

No part of this publication may be reproduced, or stored in a retrieval system, or transmitted in any form or by any means, electronic, mechanical, photocopying, recording, or otherwise, without written permission of the publisher. For information regarding permission, write to Scholastic Inc., Attention: Permissions Department, 557 Broadway, New York, NY 10012.

ISBN 0-439-28978-5

"It's a beautiful day," Cleo said. "Let's play tag in the woods."

"Uh...I don't think so,"
Clifford said. "Don't you know
about Stinky the Skunk Ghost?"

"They say he haunts the woods!" T-Bone said.

"He's twenty feet tall.
And he smells as bad as
twenty regular skunks!"

"That's just a story,"

Cleo said.

"Don't you know

Stinky isn't real?"

"Of course we do,"
Clifford said.

"Then what are we
waiting for?" Cleo said.
"Clifford, you be It."

Cleo and T-Bone ran into the woods.

Clifford ran after them.

Cleo was fast....

But Clifford was faster.

He reached out to tag her.

"Look out behind you!" Cleo shouted.

Clifford stopped in his tracks.

So did T-Bone.

"What?" they asked.

"It's Stinky the Skunk
Ghost!" Cleo cried.
Clifford and T-Bone
spun around.
But no one was
behind them.

Cleo fell over laughing.

"I fooled you!"

"That's not funny,"

said T-Bone.

"You scared us."

"I'm sorry," Cleo said.

"But you guys *know*

Stinky's not real.

Let's go swimming."

SPLISH!

SPLASH!

The dogs jumped
into the pond.

"Where is Cleo?"

Clifford asked suddenly.

"She was here a minute

ago," T-Bone said.

Just then, Cleo cried

out from the woods.

"Help! Stinky the Skunk Ghost

has got me!"

Clifford and T-Bone

ran to the rescue.

They found Cleo all alone—

alone and laughing.

"You fooled us again!"

Clifford yelped.

"That wasn't nice."

"It was a joke," Cleo said.

Clifford and T-Bone

were not amused.

They turned

and walked away.

"Don't be mad,"

Cleo called after them.

"I'm sorry."

Cleo tried to catch up

with her friends.

But her bow got caught

on a branch.

"Help!" Cleo cried.

Clifford and T-Bone

kept walking.

They thought Cleo was

playing another trick.

Then they heard
her cry out again.
Cleo sounded really scared.
And something smelled
really bad.

"P-U!" Clifford said.

"That must be Stinky.

I bet he has Cleo."

Clifford and T-Bone

ran back into the woods.

A skunk *did* have Cleo.

But this was no ghost.

This skunk was real—very real.

He left his stinky smell,

then walked away.

T-Bone held his nose
while Clifford set
Cleo free.

"Thanks, guys," Cleo said.

"I'm sorry I played

those tricks on you."

Cleo ran home

and had a bath.

Then she went to

find her friends.

"I'll never trick you again,"

she promised.

"I've learned my lesson—

the stinky way."

Do You Remember?

Circle the right answer.

1. What game did Cleo want to play in the woods?
   a. hide-and-seek
   b. baseball
   c. tag

2. Clifford and T-Bone are scared of…
   a. a bird.
   b. Stinky the Skunk Ghost.
   c. the dark.

Which happened first?
Which happened next?
Which happened last?
Write a 1, 2, or 3 in the space after each sentence.

Clifford and T-Bone jumped
into the pond.   _____

Cleo got her bow caught on
a branch.   _____

Clifford, Cleo, and T-Bone
arrived at the park.   _____

Answers:

Clifford, Cleo, and T-Bone arrived at the park. (1)
Cleo got her bow caught on a branch. (3)
Clifford and T-Bone jumped into the pond. (2)
2. b
1. c

Clifford THE BIG RED DOG®

THE RUNAWAY RABBIT

Adapted by Teddy Margulies

Drawings by Carolyn Bracken
Color by Sandrina Kurtz

**Based on the Scholastic book series
"Clifford The Big Red Dog"
by Norman Bridwell**

From the television script
"A Bunny in a Haystack"
by Anne-Marie Perrotta and Tean Schultz

SCHOLASTIC INC.

New York   Toronto   London   Auckland   Sydney   Mexico City
New Delhi   Hong Kong   Buenos Aires

ISBN 0-439-21361-4

"Wally, this is Clifford,"

Emily Elizabeth said.

"Clifford, this is Wally.

Wally is our classroom
bunny," Emily Elizabeth explained.
"It's my turn to take care
of him this weekend."

"But I have to go out now,"

Emily Elizabeth said.

"Will you stay home and watch Wally?"

Clifford wagged his

tail and woofed.

"Thanks," Emily Elizabeth said.

And she waved good-bye.

Cleo and T-Bone
came to visit.
Clifford introduced
them to Wally.

"He is so cute,"
Cleo said. "Can we
take him out
and play with him?"

"Why not?" Clifford said.

"How much trouble can

a little bunny be?"

He opened the cage.

Wally wrinkled his nose.

He wiggled his ears.

Hippity-hop!

Off he went.

Wally hopped off the table.

He hopped across the floor.

Hippity-hop!

And off he went.

Clifford and his friends

dashed after him.

Wally hopped across

the yard and into

a hollow log.

T-Bone followed him.

Wally hopped out

the other end.

But T-Bone got stuck

inside the log.

There was only one
thing to do.
Clifford took a
deep breath and...

WHOOSH!

Out popped T-Bone.

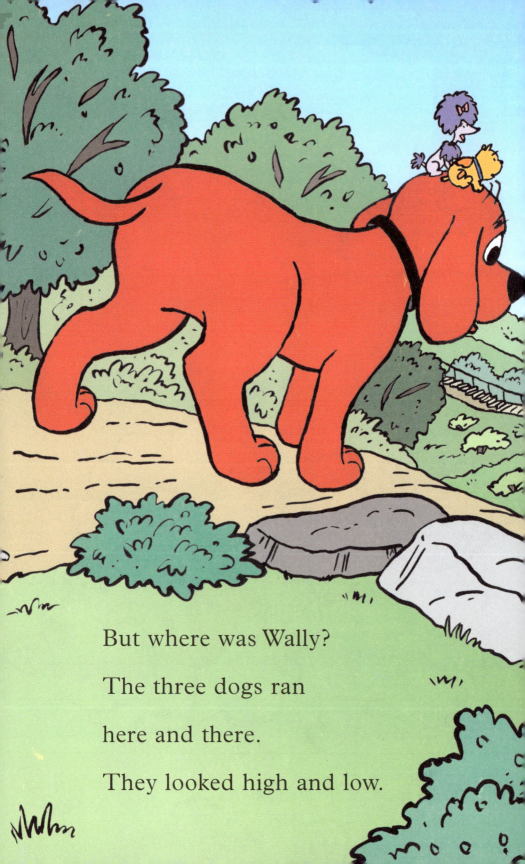

But where was Wally?

The three dogs ran

here and there.

They looked high and low.

"There he is,"

Clifford said.

"There he *was!*"

Cleo said. "Gosh,

he's fast!"

Clifford, Cleo, and

T-Bone ran as fast

as they could.

But Wally was faster.

"Where did he go?"

T-Bone asked.

"I don't know,"

Clifford said.

"But I know where I
would go if *I* were
a rabbit," he added.

Clifford, Cleo, and

T-Bone raced to

Farmer Green's.

And there was Wally.

"He'll never want to
leave here," Cleo said.
"And I'm too tired to
catch and carry him."

"We may not be able
to catch Wally,"
Clifford said.
"But we *can* catch
a carrot."

Wally followed Clifford

all the way home.

Clifford led Wally
back to his cage.
Then he gave him
the carrot.

"I never thought a
little bunny could be
so much trouble,"
Cleo said.

Just then Emily Elizabeth
came home.

"Thanks for watching
Wally," she said.

"Poor Wally has been

cooped up in his cage

all day. I think I'll let him out."

Emily Elizabeth opened the door.

"Why don't you guys play

with him while I clean

his cage!" she said.

"After all, how much trouble can a little bunny be?"

Do You Remember?

Circle the right answer.

1. Wally belonged to . . .

   a. Emily Elizabeth's best friend.

   b. Grandma.

   c. Emily Elizabeth's class.

2. Clifford, Cleo, and T-Bone found Wally . . .

   a. at the movie theater.

   b. at Farmer Green's.

   c. at Farmer Brown's.

Which happened first?
Which happened next?
Which happened last?
Write a 1, 2, or 3 in the space
after each sentence.

Clifford led Wally home with a carrot. _____

Wally ran away. _____

Emily Elizabeth asked Clifford
to watch Wally. _____

Answers:

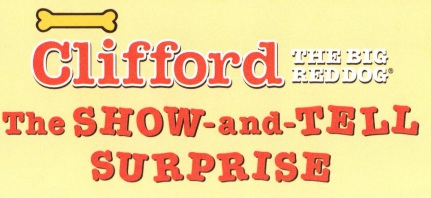

Clifford THE BIG RED DOG®

The SHOW-and-TELL SURPRISE

Adapted by Teddy Margulies

Illustrated by Steve Haefele

Based on the Scholastic book series "Clifford The Big Red Dog" by Norman Bridwell

From the television script
"My Best Friend" by Lois Becker and Mark Stratton

Cartwheel
·B·O·O·K·S·®

SCHOLASTIC INC.

New York   Toronto   London   Auckland   Sydney   Mexico City
New Delhi   Hong Kong   Buenos Aires

ISBN 0-439-21359-2

Emily Elizabeth looked
up from her desk.
She heard a rumble.
She felt the room shake.

Emily Elizabeth knew what that meant.

So did everyone in her class.

"Here comes Clifford,"

they all yelled.

"It's time to go home."

"Don't forget. Monday
is show-and-tell,"
Miss Carrington said.

"I am going to bring
something cool from
Jamaica," Charley said.

"I am going to bring

something really special,"

Jetta boasted.

Emily Elizabeth did not say
anything. She did not know
what to bring.

Emily Elizabeth and Clifford

went to the beach

to look for something

special.

While Emily Elizabeth looked,

Clifford dug.

He dug and he dug.

And he dug!

"What a special anchor!"

Emily Elizabeth said.

"My class will love it."

Jetta sniffed.

"That is just like the anchor I brought for show-and-tell *last* year."

"Oh, Clifford," Emily Elizabeth sighed.

"We must find something

special on this beach."

Then Emily Elizabeth looked down.

And Clifford looked up.

Up, up, up!

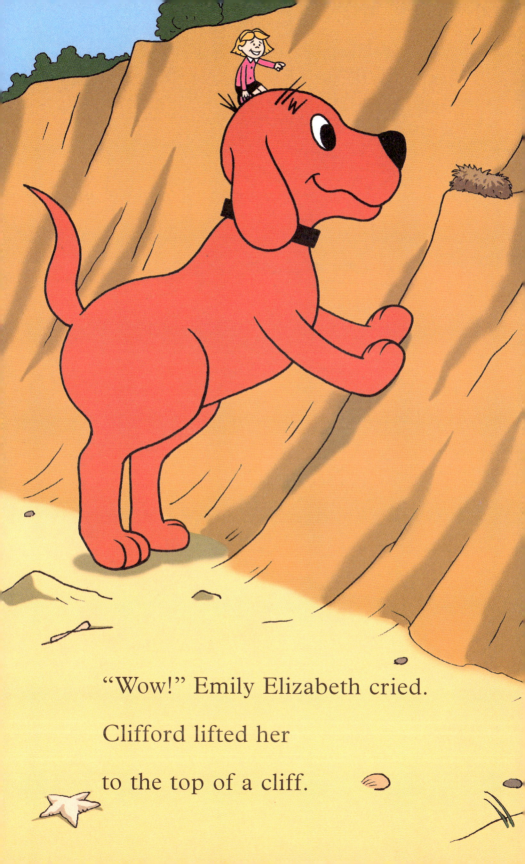

"Wow!" Emily Elizabeth cried.

Clifford lifted her

to the top of a cliff.

On the cliff was
an old nest.
It still had some feathers
and eggshells inside.

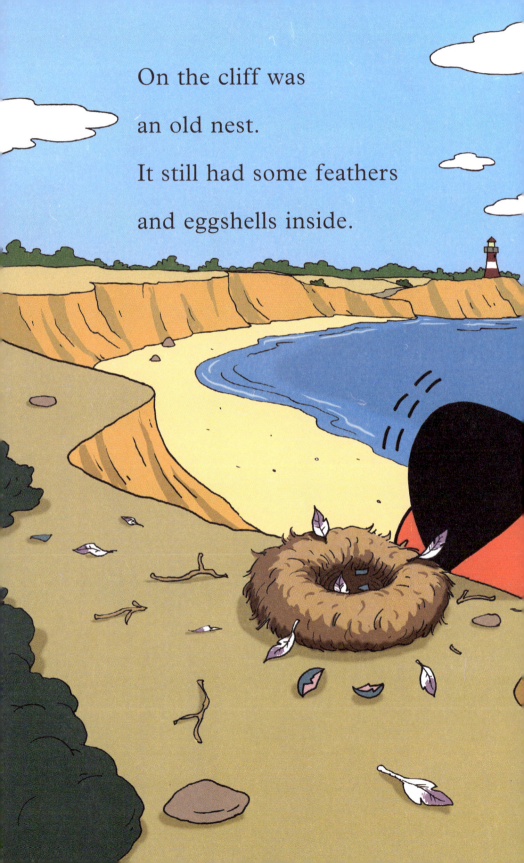

"This will be great for
show-and-tell," Emily Elizabeth said.
Clifford said, "Woof!"
and poked his nose
into the nest.

"Oh, no," Emily Elizabeth said.

Then she giggled.

Clifford looked so funny.

Emily Elizabeth left the beach
and went to town.
"Maybe Mom has something
special in her shop,"
she told Clifford.

Emily Elizabeth came out of

the shop with a coral necklace.

But it wasn't as special as

Jetta's coral statue.

Emily Elizabeth felt like crying.

But she laughed

when she saw what

Clifford was doing.

"Come on," she said.

"Let's get a snack."

Emily Elizabeth saw Charley.

"Did you find something

for show-and-tell?"

Emily Elizabeth asked him.

"I'm bringing my steel drum," he said. "What are you bringing?"

"I don't know," Emily Elizabeth said.
"Clifford and I spent the whole day
looking for something.

"We went swinging

and cliff-climbing

and shopping
in town.
But we did not find
anything special."

"That sounds like fun, though,"

Charley said. "Clifford is a cool dog."

"He sure is," Emily Elizabeth said.

"Well, I hope you
find something
for show-and-tell,"
Charley said.

"Thanks," Emily Elizabeth
said. "I think I just did."

On Monday, Emily Elizabeth
showed up for show-and-tell.
She was not alone.
"Hooray! It's Clifford!"
everyone cheered.

But Jetta did not.

"I knew you would bring

that big old red dog,"

she said.

Emily Elizabeth grinned.

"Of course," she said.

"Clifford is really special!"

Do You Remember?

Circle the right answer.

1. What was in the nest?
   - a. Peanut butter and jelly.
   - b. Feathers and seashells.
   - c. Feathers and eggshells.

2. What did Clifford and Emily Elizabeth do in town?
   - a. They went shipping.
   - b. They went chopping.
   - c. They went shopping.

Which happened first?
Which happened next?
Which happened last?
Write a 1, 2, or 3 in the space after each sentence.

Emily Elizabeth brought Clifford to show-and-tell. _____

Clifford dug a hole. _____

Clifford found an anchor. _____

Answers:

Clifford THE BIG RED DOG®

THE STORMY DAY RESCUE

Adapted by Kimberly Weinberger

Illustrated by Del and Dana Thompson

**Based on the Scholastic book series
"Clifford The Big Red Dog"
by Norman Bridwell**

From the television script
"Stormy Weather" by Bruce Talkington and Dev Ross

SCHOLASTIC INC.

New York   Toronto   London   Auckland   Sydney   Mexico City
New Delhi   Hong Kong   Buenos Aires

One day, Clifford found

a very big bone.

"I will bury it," Clifford said.

Cleo and T-Bone helped

him find a good spot.

Not far away,

Samuel was serving lunch.

"It looks as if we might

get a storm," he said.

Just then, sand began to fly.

"I asked for a fish

sandwich," said Victor,

"not a *sand*

sandwich!"

Samuel looked down.

He saw Clifford digging.

"You are getting sand

in the food!" said Samuel.

Clifford was sorry.

"Please go dig somewhere

else," Samuel said.

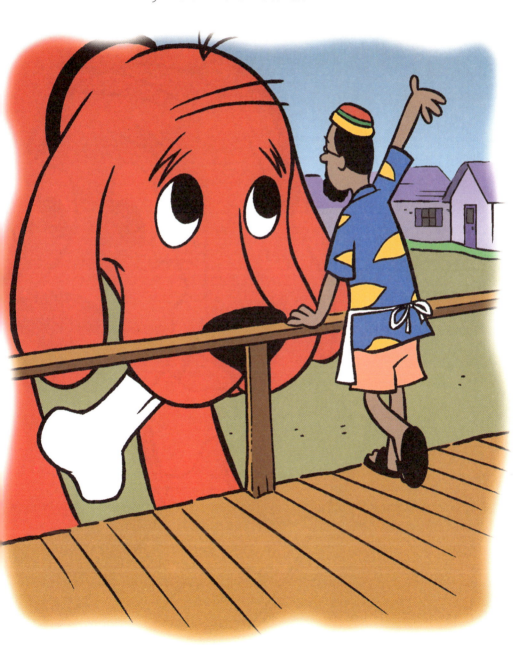

Soon Clifford, Cleo, and
T-Bone found a better spot
for the bone.

"You don't even

have to dig," said T-Bone.

"The hole is already there."

But the hole

was not deep enough

for the bone.

Clifford dug deeper.

When he finished,

Mr. Howard came to the hole.

He dropped a tree inside.

It fell to the bottom.

"How did this hole

get so deep?"

asked Mr. Howard.

Clifford barked happily.

"That hole was for this tree!"

Mr. Howard said.

"Please go dig somewhere else."

Meanwhile, the storm
grew closer.
At the school,
Miss Carrington's class
was worried.

"Remember when the last storm flooded the library?" Jetta said. "Maybe it will happen again."

"Maybe the wind

will blow things around,"

said Charley. "Like that!"

The class looked outside.

Dirt was flying everywhere!

"Clifford!" called Emily Elizabeth.

"You can't dig a hole here,"

said Emily Elizabeth.

"We are having a class."

Clifford hung his head.

Emily Elizabeth patted Clifford's nose.

"You had better go home now,"

she said.

Clifford decided

to bury his bone

in his own backyard.

He said good-bye

to Cleo and T-Bone.

Next door,

Mr. and Mrs. Bleakman

worked in their garden.

The Bleakmans

were covering their flowers

to save them from

the storm.

Clifford began to dig.

Dirt flew into

the Bleakman's yard.

Poor Clifford was told

to dig somewhere else—again.

The storm was moving closer.

Everyone met at the library.

They began to build a wall of dirt.

It would keep the waves out

during the storm.

"We have to make the wall
very high," said Mr. Howard.
"That's a lot of digging!"
said Charley.

"I know the best digger around!"
cried Emily Elizabeth. "Clifford!"

"Dig, boy," Emily Elizabeth said.

But Clifford would not dig.

Clifford just sat.

Emily Elizabeth understood.

"All digging isn't bad," she said.

"It's just that there's a right time

and place for it."

Before long, the wall was built.

Clifford saved the library!

Later, everyone gave

Clifford bones

for his hard work.

"I'll help you bury them,"

Emily Elizabeth said.

"Somewhere perfect—just like you!"

Do You Remember?

Circle the right answer.

1. What did Clifford want to bury?
   a. a toy
   b. a bone
   c. a shoe

2. Everyone was afraid _____ would flood in the storm.
   a. the school
   b. Clifford's doghouse
   c. the library

Which happened first?
Which happened next?
Which happened last?
Write a 1, 2, or 3 in the space after each sentence.

Clifford dug in his own backyard. _____

Emily Elizabeth sent
Clifford home.   _____

Clifford helped build the wall. _____

Answers:

Clifford helped build the wall. (3)
Emily Elizabeth sent Clifford home. (1)
Clifford dug in his own backyard. (2)
1-b; 2-c.

Clifford THE BIG RED DOG®
TUMMY TROUBLE

Adapted by Josephine Page

Illustrated by Ken Edwards

Based on the Scholastic book series "Clifford The Big Red Dog" by Norman Bridwell

From the television script
"Tummy Trouble" by Lois Becker and Mark Stratton

SCHOLASTIC INC.

New York   Toronto   London   Auckland   Sydney   Mexico City
New Delhi   Hong Kong   Buenos Aires

No part of this publication may be reproduced, or stored in a retrieval system, or transmitted in any form or by any means, electronic, mechanical, photocopying, recording, or otherwise, without written permission of the publisher. For information regarding permission, write to Scholastic Inc., Attention: Permissions Department, 557 Broadway, New York, NY 10012.

ISBN 0-439-21358-4

"Today you will do a trick
for your treat," Emily Elizabeth
said to Clifford.

She held up a treat

for Clifford to sniff.

"Down, Clifford," she said.

Clifford lay down.

Then he sat up,

opened his mouth,

and waited for his treat.

Emily Elizabeth tossed the treat

into Clifford's mouth.

"Good boy," she said.

"Roll over."

Clifford rolled over.

He rolled and rolled.

Then he sat up,

opened his mouth,

and waited for his treat.

Cleo and T-Bone walked by.

"Why are you sitting like that?"

Cleo asked.

"I am waiting for Emily Elizabeth to give me a treat," Clifford said. "I did a trick for her."

"I saw Emily Elizabeth

in her mother's car,"

said T-Bone.

"They drove away."

"I will give you a treat,"

said Cleo.

Cleo gave Clifford a treat.

She gave T-Bone a treat.

And she gave herself a treat.

"You have to do a trick

for your treat," Clifford said.

T-Bone stood

on his hind legs.

"That was very special,"

Cleo said.

She tossed a second treat

to T-Bone.

"That was a good toss,"

T-Bone said.

Cleo gave herself a treat

for her good toss.

"You will get sick

if you eat too many treats,"

Clifford said.

"Thank you for worrying

about me," said Cleo.

"That was very special.

You should get another treat."

T-Bone chased his tail.

Cleo tossed him a treat

and gave herself a treat

for her good toss.

Clifford walked

on his front paws.

Everyone got a treat

for that.

Clifford and T-Bone

did many more tricks.

Cleo tossed more treats.

The whole box of treats

was empty!

"Don't worry," said Cleo.
"We still have two boxes
full of treats."

"My tummy hurts,"
said T-Bone.
"Mine hurts, too,"
said Clifford.

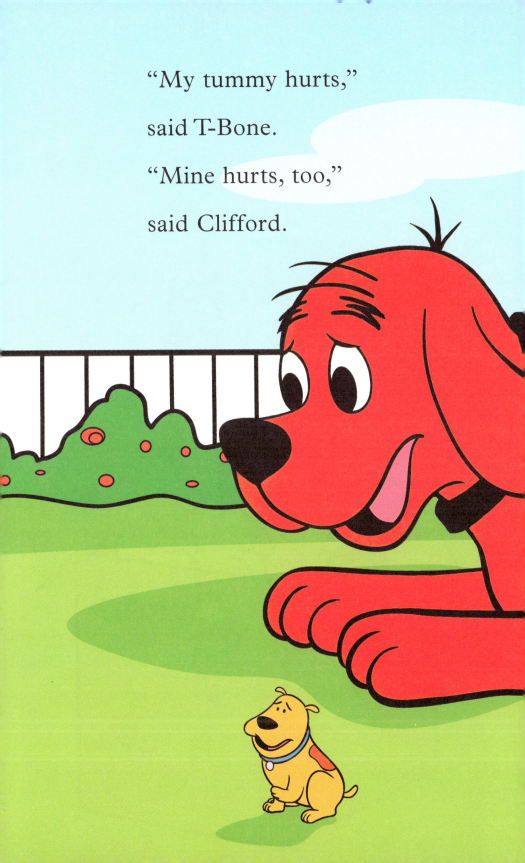

"You are probably hungry,"
said Cleo. "Have some
more treats."

Soon two boxes of treats

were empty.

Then three boxes of treats

were empty.

T-Bone lay on his back.

"I'm full," said Cleo,

who had a very big tummy.

"Me, too," said T-Bone,

who had an even bigger tummy.

"Me, three," said Clifford.

He had the biggest tummy

of all.

Emily Elizabeth came back
with treats for Clifford
and his friends.
She saw the three
empty boxes.

She saw the three

sick dogs.

"Poor doggies," she said.

"You shouldn't have

eaten all those treats.

But everybody makes

mistakes sometimes—

even the biggest, reddest,

best dog in the world.

I love you, Clifford."

Do You Remember?

Circle the right answer.

1. One of the animals walked on his or her front paws. It was...
    a. Cleo.
    b. T-Bone.
    c. Clifford.

2. Clifford felt sick because...
    a. he had a cold.
    b. he ate too much.
    c. he ate a bad apple.

Which happened first?
Which happened next?
Which happened last?
Write a 1, 2, or 3 in the space
after each sentence.

Cleo gave Clifford a treat. _____

Emily Elizabeth drove away
with her mom. _____

Emily Elizabeth saw the
three empty boxes. _____

Answers: